This Bing book belongs to:

....

Copyright © 2021 Acamar Films Ltd

The *Bing* television series is created by Acamar Films and Brown Bag Films
and adapted from the original books by Ted Dewan.

Merry Christmas, Bing! is based on the original story *Presents* written by Matthew Leys,
Mikael Shields and Claire Jennings. It was adapted from the original story by Rebecca Gerlings.

First published in Great Britain by HarperCollins *Children's Books* in 2021
HarperCollins *Children's Books* is a division of HarperCollins*Publishers* Ltd
1 London Bridge Street, London SE1 9GF

www.harpercollins.co.uk

HarperCollins*Publishers*
1st Floor, Watermarque Building, Ringsend Road, Dublin 4, Ireland

1 3 5 7 9 10 8 6 4 2

ISBN: 978-0-00-842068-0

Printed in Italy

MIX
Paper from
responsible sources
FSC® C007454

This book is produced from independently certified FSC™ paper
to ensure responsible forest management.

For more information visit: www.harpercollins.co.uk/green

Merry Christmas, Bing!

HarperCollins *Children's Books*

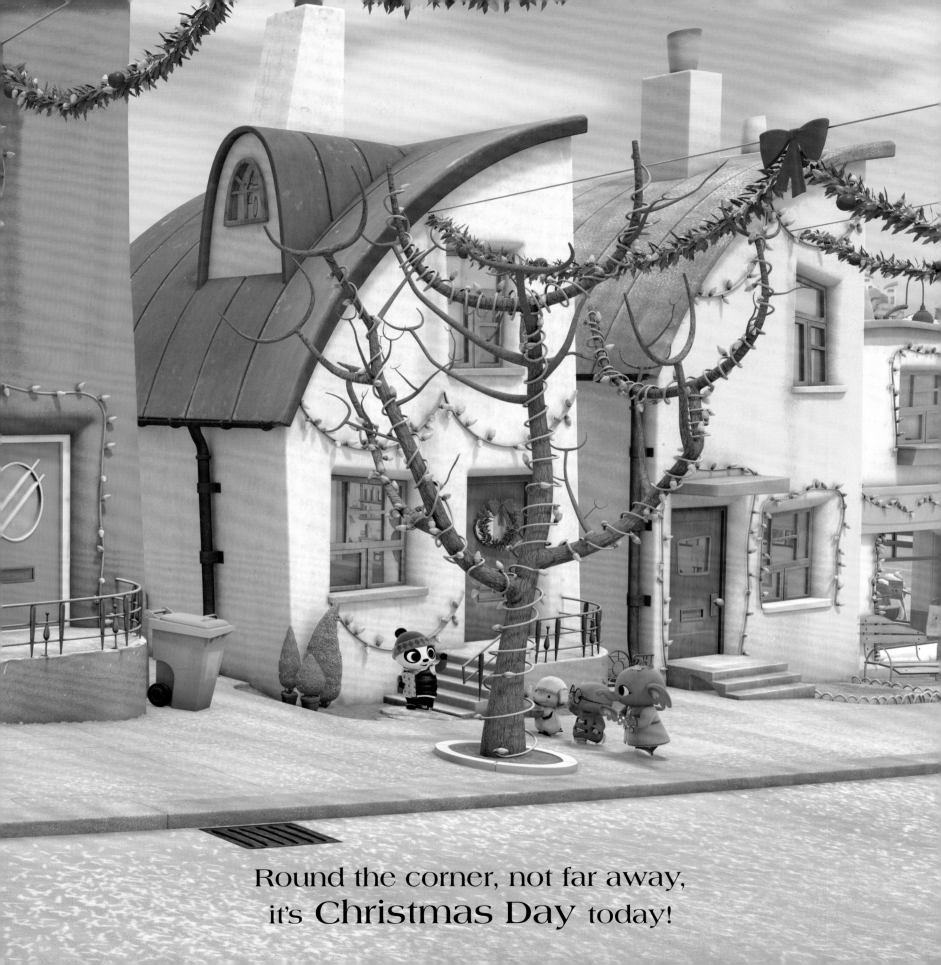

Round the corner, not far away,
it's **Christmas Day** today!

Bing is helping Flop put presents under the Christmas tree.

"Is this one mine?" asks Bing.

"No, Bing," laughs Flop. "Yours is the big yellow one."

"Is it a Hoppity Rocket Sledge?" asks Bing.

"When everyone gets here you can open it and find out," says Flop.

"I **really, really** do want a Hoppity Rocket Sledge!" says Bing.

Ding-dong!

At last, the doorbell rings and Bing vooshes to answer the door.

"Hoppity Voooooosh!"

"Ohh, merry Christmas, Bing!"

"Hello, everyone!" Bing replies.

"I've got you a present, Bing," says Sula.

Amma holds out a red dish. "And I've got your favourite Christmas carroty bake," she adds.

"Look at all these presents!"
exclaims Flop.

"Can we open them now?"
asks Bing excitedly.

Everyone crowds around the tree.

"Who's going to give out the presents?" Coco asks.

Bing knows who all the presents are for. "That present is for Flop," he explains. "And this one's for Sula . . ."

"Well, it looks like you'll need . . . the Present Hat!"
says Amma, putting it on Bing's head.

It's Bing's turn to choose the presents!

Bing reaches for his own **big yellow present.**

"We need to make sure that *everyone* has a present, Bing," reminds Flop.

"Oh, OK . . . this is for you, Sula," replies Bing, handing Sula a round present wrapped in starry paper.

"Thank you, Bing!" says Sula as she opens her present to find a beautiful orange with Bing's drawings on it. "I love it!"

"Me now!" shouts Pando as he pulls
the Present Hat on to his head.

This makes everyone laugh!

Bing helps Pando
find Flop's present.

It's a picture!
"I made it for you.
That's you and Hoppity,"
explains Bing. "Happy
Christmas, Flop!"

"Oh . . . thank
you, Bing!"

It's Nicky's turn to wear the Present Hat now.

"Nicky! Present!" he says, hugging Bing's big yellow gift.

Bing feels worried. "That's *my* present,
Nicky," he gasps.

"Can I open it now? Please, Flop?"

Sula helps Nicky hand the
big yellow present over to Bing.

At last, Bing can unwrap it . . .
He rips the paper off quickly.

"YAY!

It's Hoppity's Rocket Sledge!
Oh, *thank you,* Flop! Thank you!"

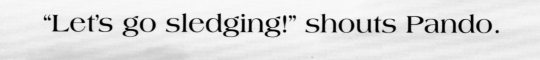

"Let's go sledging!" shouts Pando.

Everyone rushes to the window to look for SNOW . . . but there's none.

"We can't go sledging with no snow," says Coco.

Bing gazes up at the sky, sadly.

"Never mind, Bing," says Sula.
"It's still a lovely sledge!"

Everyone goes back to unwrap their presents, but Bing stays at the window.

"There isn't any snow, Flop," he sighs. "Is it going to snow today?"

"I'm afraid I don't know, Bing," replies Flop.

Amma calls over, "Flop!
We're ready for your roast potatoes!"

"Of course," answers Flop. "Come on, Bing!
Are you ready for Christmas lunch?"

Ding-dong!

It's Gilly and Popsie, with Gilly's delicious mango ice cream!
And they're just in time for lunch.

"Merry Christmas! I've got a Hoppity Rocket Sledge!"
Bing shows them, proudly. "But there's no snow . . ."

"Come on, my little Christmas crackers.
Let's wash your hands," says Amma.

Bing washes his hands and is last to reach the table.

"Ehm . . . someone's in my chair,"
he tells Flop.

"It's just as well
you've got your new
**Hoppity Rocket
Sledge**, isn't it?"
says Flop.

"YAY!"

he says,
pushing the sledge
towards the table.

"Oh, yes!"
says Sula,
making a space.
"You can have
your lunch on your
sledge, Bing!"

"Yes, I'm *vooshing* on my
Hoppity Rocket Sledge
for lunch!" laughs Bing.

Everyone tucks in to their delicious Christmas lunch.
"Oh, this is very tasty," says Amma.
"Delicious!" adds Sula.

While Bing
eats his lunch,
he sees
something
through the
window . . .

He rushes to the window
for a closer look . . .

"Snow!"
he shouts.

"Look! It's
snowing!"
says Sula.
"Merry Christmas,
Bing!"

"Merry Christmas!"
replies Bing.

Christmas . . . it's *definitely* a Bing thing!